MOUNTAIN MEADOW *123*

by Caroline Stutson
illustrated by Anna-Maria L. Crum

Roberts Rinehart Publishers
Boulder, Colorado

For Jan
Mountains or sea, friends forever.
C.R.S.

For Uncle Jimmy
Whose help is always just a phone call away.
A.L.C.

Tiptoe softly
count with me...

tawny martens

one
two
three

chasing
four
gray
chickarees.

In the meadow
in the trees...

5

five

black magpies
perch
in line.

Six

fat
golden
porcupines.

Seven
orange
skipperlings.

Eight
pink sheep moths
try
their wings.

9

Nine
striped
yellow honey
bees

buzzing
through the
fireweed.

Ten
stone
bighorns

up sky high.

9

Nine
steel eagles

sweeping by.

Eight
new bluebills
hen and drake
swimming
in a turquoise
lake.

Grizzled
marmots
seven sunning.

7

6

Six
white
billy goats
out
running.

Five

tan pikas
harvest hay.

Four
quick shiners

slip
away.

Salamanders
gleaming green,

three

go
floating
down
the stream.

Two
brown
bear cubs

head for home.

One

red ladybug
alone.

Tiptoe softly
whispering...

on the mountain
it is Spring!

Published by
ROBERTS RINEHART PUBLISHERS
5455 Spine Road, Boulder, Colorado 80301

Published in the UK and Ireland by
ROBERTS RINEHART PUBLISHERS
Trinity House, Charleston Road
Dublin 6, Ireland

Distributed in the U.S. and Canada by Publishers Group West

Printed in Hong Kong